KYLA
miss.behaves
live onstage

written & illustrated by

Kyla may

PSS!
PRICE STERN SLOAN

PRICE STERN SLOAN
Published by the Penguin Group

Penguin Group (USA) Inc., 375 Hudson Street, New York, New York 10014, U.S.A. · Penguin Group (Canada), 10 Alcorn Avenue, Toronto, Ontario, Canada M4V 3B2 (a division of Pearson Penguin Canada Inc.) · Penguin Books Ltd, 80 Strand, London WC2R 0RL, England · Penguin Ireland, 25 St Stephen's Green, Dublin 2, Ireland (a division of Penguin Books Ltd) · Penguin Group (Australia), 250 Camberwell Road, Camberwell, Victoria 3124, Australia (a division of Pearson Australia Group Pty Ltd) · Penguin Books India Pvt Ltd, 11 Community Centre, Panchsheel Park, New Delhi – 110 017, India · Penguin Group (NZ), Cnr Airborne and Rosedale Roads, Albany, Auckland 1310, New Zealand (a division of Pearson New Zealand Ltd) · Penguin Books (South Africa) (Pty) Ltd, 24 Sturdee Avenue, Rosebank, Johannesburg 2196, South Africa

Penguin Books Ltd, Registered Offices: 80 Strand, London WC2R 0RL, England

Library of Congress Cataloging-in-Publication Data

May, Kyla.
  Kyla May Miss. Behaves : live onstage / written & illustrated by Kyla May.
      p. cm.
  Summary: After Kyla May daydreams about her performance as a pop star in the upcoming drama class talent show, she discovers the power of imagination.
  ISBN 0-8431-1396-0 (pbk.) -- ISBN 0-8431-1597-1 (hardcover)
  (1. Imagination--Fiction. 2. Self-confidence--Fiction. 3. Talent shows--Fiction. 4. Schools-- Fiction.) I. Title: Kyla May Miss.Behaves : live onstage. II. Title: Kyla May misbehaves : live onstage. III. Title.

PZ7.M4535Kyl 2005
(E)--dc22
                                                                    2004026574

(pbk) 10 9 8 7 6 5 4 3 2 1
(hc) 10 9 8 7 6 5 4 3 2 1

HELLO, IT'S ME AGAIN...
KYLA MAY! What'z up?

i can't tell U how T☺TALLY excited i am! ☺
2morrow is our 'Performing Arts Festival', which is a
fancy name 4 my **Drama class's** annual *talent show*.
In fact, i'm IN **Drama class** now, which is, like, my
absolute FAVE class EVER.

Ms. Shakespeare
is my **Drama** teacher &
without a doubt the
C☺☺LEST teacher **i** know.
(i hope i'm as cool as she
is when i grow up.)
Like, she totally gets ME.
She also has a WiLD
imagination & is super
CREATIVE...just like ME !

I TOTALLY get YOU!

C my special dictionary @ back of journal!

(Wonder if Ms. Shakespeare's related 2 William Shakespeare, the Englishman
who wrote some of the world's most famous plays ever hundreds of yrs ago —
ever heard of Romeo & Juliet? Hamlet? He wrote 'em.)

Let me explain more about 2morrow's awesome _talent show_...each student will have 3 minutes 2 perform in front of the entire class. It can B anything "entertaining," highlighting our natural abilities. (Hmmm...where does someone like ME start?!!!)

Ms. Shakespeare & 2 other teachers will judge the best _talent_. 1 person will win (which of course will B ME! Like, really now...who else?)

Distressingly, last year, Bianca Boticelli (my arch rival) WON! (hmmm...wonder if her dad had anything 2 do with that?) Bianca TOTALLY upstaged EVERYONE with a gymnastics routine that included hula hoops, flashing juggling balls & her dog Gemima, the infamous Pug. (Don't worry, Fifi-belle – she's no way as cool as U.)

of course she's not!!!

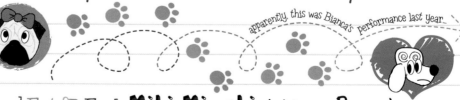

apparently, this was Bianca's performance last year...

My bEst fREnd **Miki Minski** told me Bianca's performance was, like, full-on -incredible, but unfortunately (or mayB fortunately, 4 once!) i didn't get 2 C the 'Bianca spectacle,' because i was in _detention_ !!! ☹

4

A devastating *sequence of events* resulted in ME missing out on not only watching the talent show...but also from...performing in it!!! (totally worse) ☹

...neither was I!

Now U can C why Bianca WON...'cause, like, i wasn't even there 2 UPSTAGE her! WINNERS

mayB last year...but not this year

i was going 2 *perform* a **ballet** routine from Sleeping Beauty, but tragically, in a moment of madness, i lost concentration during **Math** class a few days B4 the 'Performing Arts Festival.' (So not cool!) i was so T☺TALLY hyped about the impending *talent show* that i was practicing my routine in my head, instead of multiplying in reality. **Ms. Biggleton** didn't appreciate my dedication 2 **ballet** during **Math**!

a kyla may tip:

use my 1st journal 2 break the code

This tragedy ended with ME writing *'lines'* as punishment... DURING the 'Performing Arts Festival.' Like, can U believe it?

(memories of 1 of the worst days of my life)

A year later i'm still in TOTAL SHOCK! It may B years until i'm totally over this *trauma*. ☹ ☹ ☹ ☹ ☹ ☹

I must always concentrate in class
I must always concentrate in class
I must always concentrate in class
I must always concentrate in class
I must always concentrate in class
I must always concentrate in class
I must always concentrate in class
I must always concentrate in class
I must always concentrate in class
I must always concentrate in class
I must always concentrate in class
I must always concentrate in class
I must always concentrate in class
I must always concentrate in class

i've kept the lines 2 inspire me 2 behave this year so i'll never miss the festival again.
Check 'em out!

OK, no more of that 'cause now i'm focused on being both a **SUPERSTAR** student... & a **SUPERSTAR** on stage!

♡ i can't wait 2 tell U about my performance 4 2morrow's competition. Actually B4 i tell U about that, let me tell U how i decided which talent 2 perform, 'cause, like, i have SO many! ☺

Ballet?

Acting?

Singing?

Performance Art?

Hmmm... which TALENT?

Disco Dancing?

Poetry?

Initially **i** was going 2 do **ballet**. But 2 B honest, i'm a little 'over' **ballet** @ the moment. Like, 4 the last **6 yrs ballet** has been my no. 1 obsession, after daydreaming, of course. & i feel it's time 2 have a NEW obsession.

...i started taking **ballet lessons** when i was 5. **Mum** dropped ME off @ my 1st class, which fully changed my life 4ever.

Like, it was SOOOOO unreal! i TOTALLY felt magical — i was in **ballet class**, but in my imagination, i was dancing in an enchanted forest & then a royal palace. 'Cause in **ballet**, U must pretend 2 B a swan or a princess dancing in a beautiful setting. No wonder i was obsessed. My imagination was working overtime.

...tell me about it! she was in her element!!!

← wasn't i totally cute!

Kyla May - 5 yrs old

Everyone *thinks* **ballet** is complicated, but it's not if U know the **5 basic positions** of your FEET.

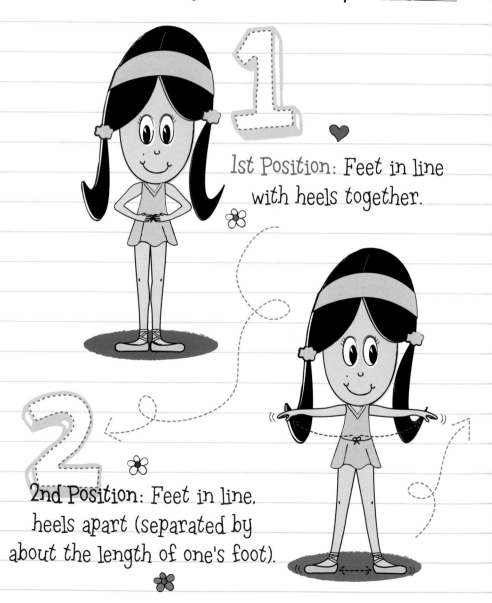

1st Position: Feet in line with heels together.

2nd Position: Feet in line, heels apart (separated by about the length of one's foot).

3rd Position: Feet touching, 1 foot in front of the other & overlapping by about $\frac{1}{2}$ the length of the foot.

4th Position: Feet apart, separated about the length of a foot, 1 foot in front of the other.

5th Position: Feet touching, 1 foot in front, heel 2 toe & toe 2 heel.

Is this 5th position?

Here's a photo from my **ballet recital** last year.
My **ballet** school did 'The Nutcracker,' which is a
famous **ballet** about Christmas toys coming 2 life.
(Like, HELLO!, my toys always come 2 life! There4 i
could T☺TALLY relate.)

i had the main part — a girl named CLARA. i was
awesome, so awesome that, in a way, i was the BEST
i could ever B. i peaked. Now, 4 some reason, **ballet** isn't
as exhilarating anymore. ☹

You were the BEST!

The Nutcracker ballet is based on the story "The Nutcracker and the Mouse King" written by E.T.A Hoffmann. In 1891, Tchaikovsky, the famous composer, was commissioned 2 write the music 4 the Nutcracker ballet. The Nutcracker was 1st danced in 1892, in Russia.

Like...how incredibly gorgeous am i!!!

Mum reckons i've 'grown out' of **ballet**. (i'm not sure what she means since my **ballet** shoes still fit me.)

Dad says **ballet** no longer challenges me. He says "we must always challenge ourselves, otherwise life becomes boring" — & U know, i don't do B☹☺☺RING

i think **Dad**'s right...& there4, 4 this year's talent show, ♡ i decided 2 go 4 a challenge.

But since ♡i still absolutely L♡♡♡♡VE 2 **DANCE** & there R like a gazillion different dance styles, i pondered over doing a few.

i 1st thought about the **cancan...**

MOULIN ROUGE CANCAN

(The cancan is a traditional French dance that has been performed @ the famous Moulin Rouge in Paris 4 way more than 100 years.)

...then **ballroom dancing**...

May I have this dance?

(This type of dancing used 2 B something our parents & grandparents...& great-grandparents did. but nowadays they have sped up the tempo & the dancing is totally cool & glamorous.)

...♡ i also considered... ★ ☆ ★ ★ ★ ★ ★ ★ ★ ☆

DISCO DANCING...

(Like, 1 of my routines...

Yeah, disco dancing... my fave!

i always perform...

2 my FAVE dance track...

...4 Mum & Dad.)

Hmmm...?

...tap dancing was a possibility, 2.

(But with all of the
jumping up & down,
tap dancing hurts
my teeth
after a while...hmmm...
Mental note: probably need 2
visit the dentist!
Should tell Mum & Dad!)

Hmmm...?

But...hey, EVERYONE KNOWS i'm incredible @ any kind
of DANCE...& i needed a challenge my classmates
wouldn't expect. (Dad also says "to always keep
'em guessing!")

So... i thought about **ACTING**. ♡ i tossed 'round the idea of doing a little SHaKeSpEARE. Like, mayB a scene from 'Romeo & Juliet'... ♥

...Call me but love...

(O Romeo, Romeo! wherefore art thou Romeo?)

Hmmm....?

which is also known as 'Improvisation'

...**Improv acting** also popped in2 my head.

Hmmm...?

(Which is a style of acting that totally uses your imagination. Sort of like full-on make believe... you just make stuff up on the spot. In this scene i am a tree swaying in the wind...)

Hmmm.. but, like, i'm 4ever performing in character as it is! That's the best thing about ME! Every day i act like someone else. With my imagination, i'm always playing different roles. ☺

There4 ACTING wasn't challenging enough either.

19

Finally!!!...i WORKED IT OUT! i found my calling...& i totally confess, it's my NEW OBSESSION!

Lately i've wanted 2 B a POP STAR when i grow up. Yes, i hear U...i know only a few weeks ago it was a DANCER,

...& B4 that a **Supermodel**

You could be anything you want!

...& last week an artist like **Mum**,

...just after an architect like **Dad**.

...but this week i'm T☺TALLY committed 2 being a POP STAR. Cross my heart...

gorgeous

rhythmic

role-model

unreal voice

fashion-guru

visionary

pop star

Like, i have all the necessary qualities...i'm gorgeous, rhythmic (i can dance circles 'round anyone), i have an unreal voice, role-model qualities (everyone looks up 2 me...& it's not just 'cause i'm tall 4 my age!), i'm a fashion guru, visionary (which means i can C in2 the future, predict trends)...Basically...i could B the next big thing!

i'm totally POP-IDOL material.

This recent desire 2 B a POP STAR began the other night with a dream...or let's call it a VISION of my sensational future.

of course i'm the lead singer

POP STAR

this is my vision

...i imagined i was discovered in a band - not a brass band but a hip & funky ROCK BAND that rehearses every day after school in someone's garage. (Hmmm...if i want this dream 2 come true, i better stop getting detention so i don't miss rehearsals!) ☹

i **dreamt** that a record producer happened 2 B walking past the garage 1 afternoon & heard our totally C☺☺L ROCK sound & was fully blown away.

That money will buy a lot of presents for me!

The record producer recognized MY TALENT & offered ME a $1 million dollar record contract!!!

I agree to the terms of this $1,000,000.00 record contract.

signed

kyla may

kyla may

Like, how T☺TALLY awesome would that B!? ☺

i was a total **overnight success**, well, like over a few **nights** 'cause it took **Mum** & **Dad** a few nights 2 accept my new career path. (Hey...when talent comes knocking...what do ya do? Answer the door, of course!)

Being a 'rock diva,' i needed a ROCK name. The record company totally liked my existing nickname 'MS. BEHAVES.' Unreeeeeeal!

but they changed 'miss.' 2 'ms.' 2 B politically correct...or "P.C."

My look was a 'PUNK'D -UP beauty queen.' (A totally hip stylist gave me a fantabulous makeover!)

introducing... MS. BEHAVES

rock diva

MS. BEHAVES

AFTER

BEFORE

Fifi-belle changed her look 2, since **French Poodles** don't exactly say 'ROCK 'N' ROLL.' The *stylist* straightened her curls & gave her a mohawk, with a new *studded leather collar.* She looked totally C☺☺L!

BEFORE

oh! I love my new look!

ROCK 'N' ROLL

Fifi would definitely scare the cats with this look!

AFTER

1st

My **1st** single was titled: "Turn Around Beauty Queen." It was a song about finding beautiful people on any street corner. Like suggesting everyone can B a total **beauty queen**.

Now, everyone knows that when you're a POP STAR, U must have a HOT video...which of course, i had. :)

In this fantabulous daydream, my video was set on the streets of New York. i was wearing a funked-up tiara & gown. i ran around the streets finding "drab" people... & giving them makeovers, turning them in2 beauty queens, or as i call 'em..."fab" people.

wide shot: we open on Ms.B walking along street, pan along graffiti wall

city skyline in background

C/U of Ms.B – singing begins

Ms.B approaches "drab" person

C/U of "drab" person

SFX: fast forward action as Ms.B
does makeover — movement blurred

SFX: fast forward — C/U

From
drab to
fab...I
love it!

pull back 2 reveal
a beauty queen

crowds appear, v. impressed with
transformation.
POV: someone in crowd

C/U of Ms.B — she is
v. satisfied with her makeover

fade out 2
NYC skyline @ sunset

pretty cool, right?

Prod: Music Video
artist: Ms. Behaves
song: Turn Around, Beauty Queen

ROLL:	SCENE:	TAKE:
4	7	3

Director: Simon Dinsmore

Btw: Ms. B = Ms. Behaves, C/U = close up,
SFX = special effects, POV = point of view

Fifi-belle also starred in my video — we cut 2 her doing daredevil jumps

on a skateboard
as she RAPPED.

MS. BEHAVES
featuring pooch-doggie-dog

pooch-doggie-dog is Fifi-belle's rap name

My song hit No. 1 on the charts. i was a sensation.

Being a POP STAR meant life totally changed...suddenly EVERYONE wanted 2 B like ME...(actually my life is already like that!) But anyway, in my dream, i became a full-on, huge 'star.' Like, i had FANS chasing me everywhere. i T☺TALLY lost my anonymity, which meant EVERYONE recognized ME. i couldn't even walk down the street 2 buy a hot chocolate without being chased & photographed by the paparazzi. ☆ ☆ ☆ ☆ ☆

Neither could FIFI-BELLE.

LIFE AS A POP STAR

ok...my real life isn't completely like this

♡ i had more No.1 HITS, 1 after the other. Which turned in2 a No.1 ALBUM.

♥ i became the "Princess of Rock," selling 1 billion copies of my self-titled album: MS. BEHAVES.

includes
no. 1 hits:
• "turn around, beauty queen"
• "not just a pretty face"
• "i must behave"
• "detention blues"

1 billion copies sold

♥ With stardom came *concerts*, world tours, a *celebrity life* & of course, an 'entourage.' btw: an 'entourage' is the *people who hang out with U*, which in this case incl. my band, personal assistant, record producer, fans (a.k.a. groupies), lawyer, spiritual guru, cook, psychic, agent, MUM & DAD, Fifi-belle, Miki & Sienna.

☺ **POP STARS** can B v. demanding when it comes 2 their dressing rooms. They *insist* on being surrounded by certain items that apparently enhance their performance. There4 in my dream, i demanded that everything in my dressing room be pink, incl. water, flowers, dressing gown, bubble bath, cookies, milkshakes, etc.

☺ dressing room checklist: ☺

☑ water

☑ flowers

☑ milkshakes

☑ bath

☑ cookies

☑ dressing gown

I'd dye myself pink if you demanded.

☺ Like, HELLO! If U were a POP STAR, i'm sure U'd do the same!

sad
face
x100

Eek!!!!! Oh NOOOOOO!!!!
i CAN'T BELIEVE what just happened! This has never
happened B4. EVER!...i just got in TROUBLE with
Ms. Shakespeare DURING **Drama class**!

Ms. Shakespeare is T☺TALLY disappointed in
ME. ☹ So am i!

oh no...
here
we go
again...

i've NEVER daydreamed that bad in **Drama** B4...but i
s'pose recalling my life as a **Pop-Diva** was v. intense.
Like, anyone could get a little carried away reliving such
an awesome experience.

As punishment, i have detention after school. Like, even though Ms. Shakespeare L♥VES me, she must teach ME a lesson.

But, oh no!!! 2nite of all nights! i totally needed another night's practice of my POP STAR routine.

☆ ☆ ☆ ☆

Oh...depression...i'm SO jealous everyone else can go HOME & rehearse...while i'm stuck HERE! What a loser ♡ i am. ☹

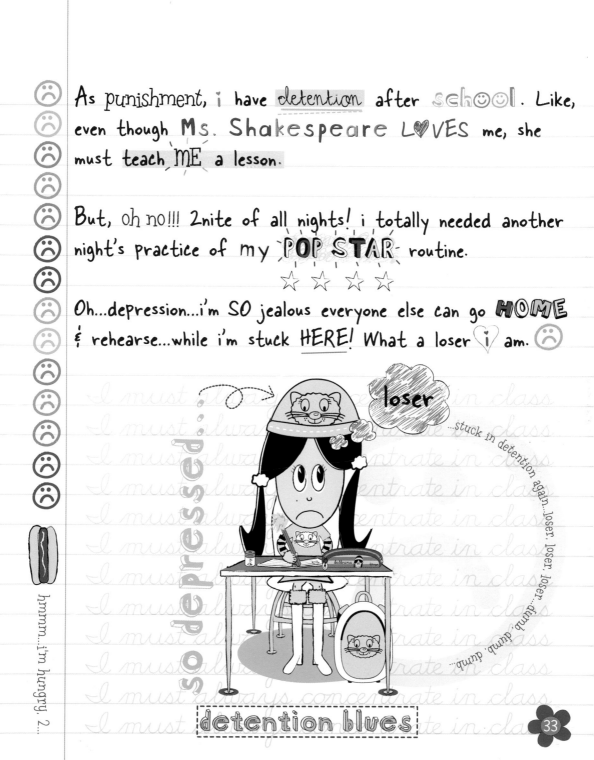

loser

...stuck in detention again...loser...loser...loser...dumb, dumb, dumb...

so depressed...

I must always concentrate in class

detention blues

Actually, i s'pose this gives ME a chance 2 tell U about my star-studded performance i've planned 4 2morrow's talent show. (i'm so determined 2 WIN...now it's my turr 2 upstage everyone else. Bianca...watch out!)

2morrow i'm singing an 'original' song. 'Original' means that i wrote it ALL BY MYSELF...yes, i know, my talents never cease! Yesterday – DANCING...2day – SONG WRITING.. (2morrow...hmmm...hopefully not detention again!)

My SONG is about being misunderstood, as i frequently suffer from this.

Through My Eyes

If U could only C the world thru my eyes
Surely then U'd realize.........

With an imagination like mine, life is divine!
But the world wants me 2 B normal - why?
Cuz that's so dull & formal
That kind of life is soooooooo wrong & so i sing this song

Hmmm...wonder how **Miki**'s act is coming along? i bet she's @ **HOME** practicing. She's performing a traditional **Russian** Polka 2morrow — a dance her **Russian** grandma taught her. i know she'll B **TOTALLY** brilliant.

Hmmm... she's very good!

miki's mum & dad watching her practice

Hmmm...& ♡ i bet Sienna's sounding *sensational*. She's singing an **Italian opera**. She fully sings like an **angel from heaven**.

Oh, i don't even want 2 think about Bianca practicing... last year GEMIMA was such a HIT, i bet she's planning an encore performance with her Pug.

SUPER STAR
Gemima

Which reminds me...i hope **Fifi-belle**'s practicing, 2. Like ME, **Fifi-belle** has an amazing voice. She'll B my backup singer 2morrow. Like, AS IF i'd do anything without her by my side! ☺

Excuse me! But I am also a super-star!!!

i ♥ fifi

Actually, i just had a realization! Why can't i practice my act in my imagination? Like, just 'cause i'm in detention doesn't mean i can't go over my performance in my head.

Hmmm...now let's C...

i must remember 2...

Wow...in my imagination...i AM BRILLIANT!!! i'm groovy. i'm fantabulous. Bring on 2morrow!

☹ Yeah! i'm FREE from detention !!!...& @ HOME @ last.
Gosh, i still haven't finalized my look 4 2morrow.
Hmmm...what shall i **wear**?

Soooooooooooo many options...

What about PUNK?...

hmmm...

* ripped clothing is essential

* tartan is the look

* black is a must

* leather 4 sure

* safety pins all over

mum
dad
me
fifi
miki
nana

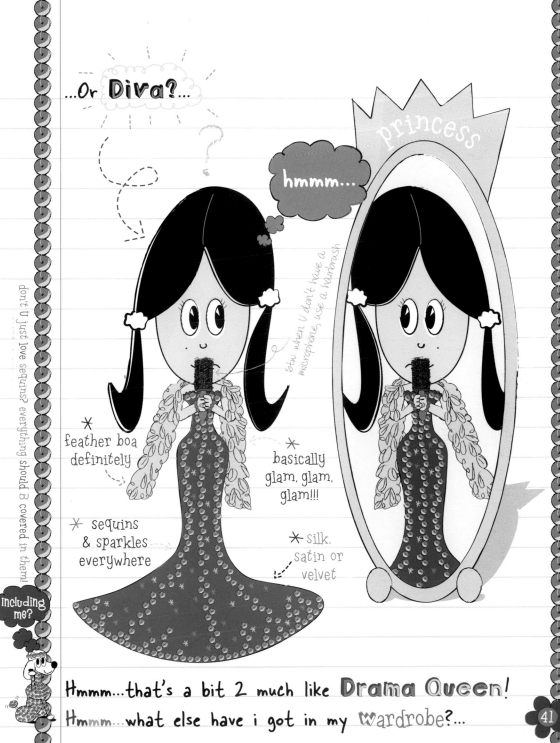

...Or **Diva?**...

hmmm...

princess

don't U just love sequins? everything should B covered in them!

including me?

* feather boa definitely

* basically glam, glam, glam!!!

* sequins & sparkles everywhere

* silk, satin or velvet

btw, when U don't have a microphone, use a hairbrush

Hmmm...that's a bit 2 much like **Drama Queen!**
Hmmm...what else have i got in my wardrobe?...

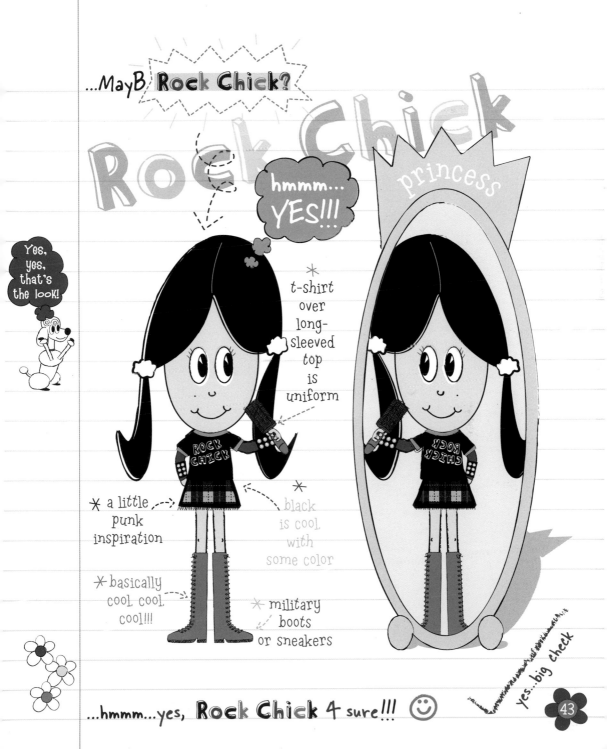

Phew! i have some time left B4 _bed_, there4 i can just get a quick **practice** in. **Fifi-BELLE**, R U ready?... _imagine_ we're performing 2morrow...

don't you just loooove my bed? Dad & i designed it!

my best friend

my puppy

my 2 best friends:
1 x human, 1 x canine

of course, Fifi sleeps with me

Stardom Skills

U R TALENTED!

how to write a hit

WOW!!!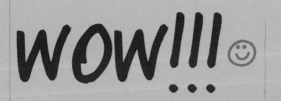

i am sooooooo HOT!!! Oops...sorry, Fifi...WE'RE HOT!

2morrow we're going 2 B HUGE! EVERYONE will
L♥♥♥♥VE & adore ME...i mean US...but, Fifi,
remember...don't upstage me!

(Knock, knock) "Kyla May, time for bed. Darling...you
have a big day tomorrow."

Oops, better get some shut-eye. Good night.

Finally the big day is here! ☺

i'm last 2 perform. (Hmmm...like, obviously they're saving the BEST 4 last!)

Miki did a fantabulous job. Her grandma was in the audience. She got SO excited @ the end of Miki's dance that she ran up onstage & nearly "squashed" Miki with a massive, scary 'grandma hug.'

Like, Hello!!! Miki's face went totally BLUE - i don't think she could breathe!!!

EEK!!!!!...someone save her from the 'grandma hug'

Sienna's operetta was excellent, 2. But @ 1 point she hit such a **high note**, i was sure the windows would shatter.

oh, the standard is very high!

(phew... close !)

me...in the audience

Gosh, the standard is v. GOOD this year.
Like, i REALLY have my work cut out 4 me.
Eek, i'm starting 2 feel a little nervous.
⭐ Bianca's next... ☹

Well, i confess Bianca's performance was TOTALLY impressive. But Gemima unquestionably took the spotlight away from her master.

Oops...Fifi-BELLE's nervous now! C'mon, Fifi-BELLE... let's get ready...

Gemima was brilliant!

☹ @ last it was MY turn 2 perform ...but 4 some reason i couldn't move!!!!!!!! ☹

i was frozen, but shaking @ the same time

OH NO!!! WHAT'S WRONG?

check out how white i was →

usual skin color

nervous-wreck skin color

ROCK CHICK

Fifi didn't understand what was going on.

This had never happened B4. i had STAGE FRIGHT ...can U believe it!?!? i was frozen...& tongue-tied. Like, my nerves totally got the better of me.

...i could only *imagine* making an enormous F☹☹L of myself. i could only picture me...

OH NO!

> ...falling offstage,

EEK!!!

> ...4getting the words,

HELP!

> ...singing off-key

NOOO!

> ...& everyone laughing @ mE !!!

Oh dear, like, i didn't know what 2 do!

isn't Kyla next?

where is she?

Ms. Shakespeare came up 2 me backstage & explained that i was JUST NERVOUS. She said i had "cold feet." (Hmmm...weird...'cause my feet seemed totally hot & sweaty — like the rest of me!)

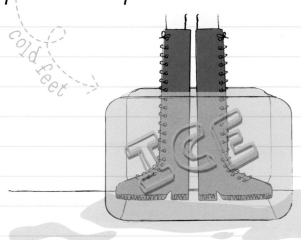

cold feet

Ms. Shakespeare explained that my self-confidence was letting me down, NOT my talent.

You are awesome in reality, too!

...promise!

i told Ms. Shakespeare just how awesome i was when i rehearsed in my head. Oh my Gosh... i then had a shocking realization... mayB it's ALL IN MY HEAD! Like, mayB in reality i wasn't any good @ all!!! ☹

it's ALL IN MY HEAD!

Ms. Shakespeare then told me about the power of our imagination ...it's a tool 2 help us dream & visualize. If we can C OURSELVES as something in our head, it's the 1st step 2 making our dreams come true.

She said i'm lucky 2 have such an amazing imagination, which is a gift of visualization (i.e., being able 2 C the future, e.g., seeing what U want 2 B when U grow up).

Your imagination can TOTALLY help U achieve your dreams in real life. Ms. Shakespeare said, "you can be anything you want to be if you believe in yourself."

She also said, "...if you can see yourself performing brilliantly in your imagination, then you can do so in reality, too."

She told me 2 B more self-confident. Which meant i had 2, like,........... "believe in myself."

@ last i had the courage 2 go onstage...& i performed SO brilliantly...AS i ALWAYS iMAGiNED! Like, EVERYONE listened & connected 2 my lyrics. After all, we're all *a little misunderstood.* 😊

i DANCED perfectly & the judges were TOTALLY impressed. EVERYONE clapped along, which made ME feel so much better. 😊

FIFI-BELLE was excellent, 2. She sang on key & didn't upstage me @ all...i'm sure i saw Gemima's tail drop during Fifi's solo performance!

Miki & Sienna were fantabulous — they encouraged ME nonstop throughout my act. & out of the corner of my eye, i saw Mum & Dad so excited. (Like, i think Dad even cried!) 😊

The crowd loved me, 2...& <u>NO ONE</u> laughed @ me — they just cheered & cheered. Hooray...i'm a total STAR!!! A full-on POP STAR! ☺

Like, even if i don't WIN, just the *experience* was T☺TALLY worth everything. However, when the judges named moi (French 4 'me') the WINNER...it made the experience a bazillion times better!!!

← oh...and Fifi, 2!

Yippeeeee! i WON!!!!!!!! i'm the most TALENTED <u>EVER</u>. (Like, no surprise there!)

Miki & Sienna raced up 2 congratulate me backstage. They were totally stoked 2, 'cause Sienna got **2nd** place, & **Miki** got **3rd**. We're all **WINNERS**! Yeah!!!

Bianca was SOOOOO jealous...she stormed off, dragging poor little **Gemima** behind her.

Mum & **Dad** almost had 2 restrain themselves from running onstage like **Miki**'s grandma. They came up after the award ceremony & told me how **PROUD** they were. By this stage **Mum** was sobbing with pride, & i'm sure i saw another tear in **Dad**'s eye!

As a reward 4 my excellent performance, **Mum** & **Dad** said i could have a **sleepover**.
Like, double Yeahhhhh x 1 million!!! Unreal x 1 billion!!!

i invited **Miki** & Sienna, of course. ☺

When we got **HOME**, **Mum & Dad** had an awesome surprise waiting...a karaoke machine! Even if i didn't **WIN**, they still wanted me 2 have it. (They R totally the C⊙⊙LEST parents EVER!)

My bEstE T fR EndS & i had so much FUN performing 4 **Mum & Dad**.

don't tell anyone...but i was 4 sure the best @ karaoke, of course!

Hmmm...mayB when i grow up i can still B a POP STAR, but instead of being a single artist, i'll B in a girl group with Miki & Sienna...hey, we could B the "Beauty Queens" ...or what about "The Miss. Behaviors"?...hmmm...mayB the "Pop Princesses"?...or the "Rock Chicks"? What an end 2 a brilliant day! ☺ ☺ ☺ ☺ ☺ ☺ ☺

like, what a totally HOT lookin' group!

2 billion copies sold

So don't 4get 2 always:

...USE YOUR IMAGINATION...

...& YOUR DREAMS WILL COME TRUE...

...& always BELIEVE IN YOURSELF.

KYLA MAY's Dictionary:

2	=	to/too
2day	=	today
2morrow	=	tomorrow
2nite	=	tonight
4	=	for
4ever	=	forever
4get	=	forget
B	=	be
B4	=	before
btw.	=	by the way
C	=	see
fantabulous	=	fantastic + fabulous
in2	=	into
mayB	=	maybe
R	=	are
there4	=	therefore
U	=	you
V.	=	very
@	=	at
&	=	and
=	=	equals

i give U permission 2 use my dictionary with your friends!

64